Christin

ANNA MARIE'S BLANKET

by

Joanne Barkan

Illustrated by Deborah Maze

BARRON'S

New York • London • Toronto • Sydney

To Jon

© Copyright 1990 by Joanne Barkan
Illustrations © Copyright 1990 by Barron's Educational Series, Inc.

All inquiries should be addressed to:
Barron's Educational Series, Inc.
250 Wireless Boulevard
Hauppauge, New York 11788

International Standard Book No. 0-8120-6124-1

Library of Congress Catalog No. 89-39195

Library of Congress Cataloging-in-Publication Data

Barkan, Joanne
Anna Marie's blanket / by Joanne Barkan; illustrated by Deborah Maze.
    p.   cm.
    Summary: A little girl's blanket resents her going off to nursery school and
leaving it behind until she assigns it the job of looking after all her other
toys while she's away.
    ISBN 0-8120-6124-1
    [1. Blankets—Fiction.] I. Maze, Deborah, ill. II. Title.
PZ7.B25039An   1990   89-39195
[E]—dc20   CIP
                                             AC

PRINTED IN HONG KONG

012   9923   987654321

"WHAT DO YOU MEAN I'M NOT GOING WITH YOU?"

Anna Marie's blanket stared angrily at Anna Marie.

"Yesterday you didn't take me when you went shopping with your dad. The day before that, your mom took you for ice cream, and you didn't invite me. And now you're going to the playground without me. *What* is going on here?"

Anna Marie looked down at her shoes and pretended to fix the laces. When she looked up, there were tears in her eyes. "It's hard to tell you this," she said. She took a deep breath. "We can't be together all the time anymore."

"WHAT?" gasped the blanket.

Anna Marie spoke quickly. She wanted to get it all out at once. "I'm starting nursery school soon, and I can't take you. Everyone says I'm too old for a blanket."

"TOO OLD FOR A BLANKET?" The blanket gasped again.

Anna Marie tried to explain. "We're still best friends—even if I don't take you everywhere. I still love you."

"I don't want to hear this," the blanket said. It flung one of its corners over the other and turned away.

Later that day, Anna Marie was bandaging her monkey's paw. Her blanket lay slumped on the floor.

Suddenly the blanket sat up and said to Anna Marie, "You're just not being fair. *I've* never gone off and left *you*, have I? Don't I sit with you all the way through dinner—even when you're having fish? Don't I stay up late and tell you jokes when you can't sleep?"

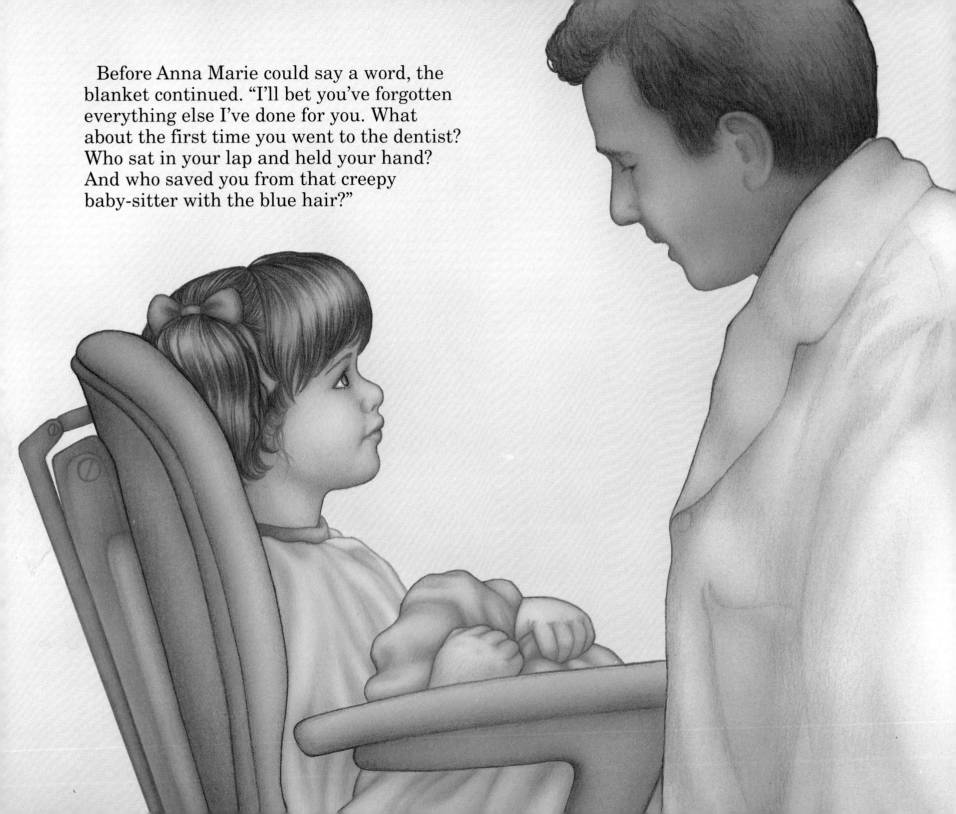

Before Anna Marie could say a word, the blanket continued. "I'll bet you've forgotten everything else I've done for you. What about the first time you went to the dentist? Who sat in your lap and held your hand? And who saved you from that creepy baby-sitter with the blue hair?"

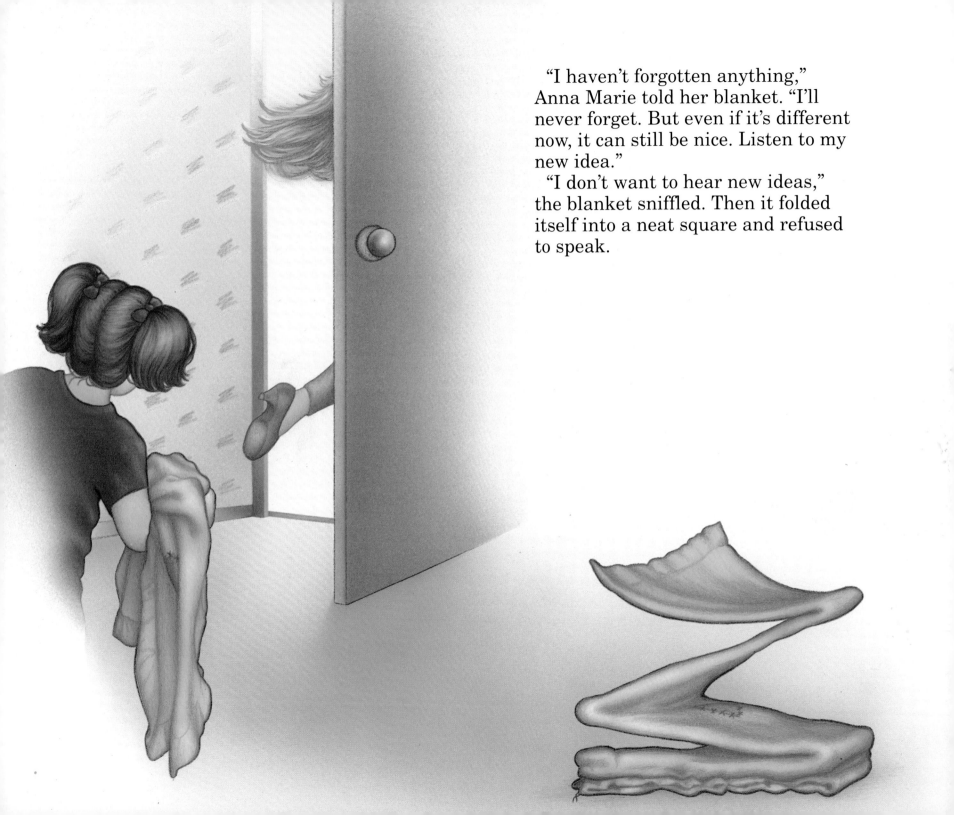

"I haven't forgotten anything," Anna Marie told her blanket. "I'll never forget. But even if it's different now, it can still be nice. Listen to my new idea."

"I don't want to hear new ideas," the blanket sniffled. Then it folded itself into a neat square and refused to speak.

The next day, while Anna Marie was feeding her rabbit, the blanket swished by. "You know," it announced, "nursery school is going to be horrible if you don't take me with you."

"Horrible?" Anna Marie asked in a surprised voice.

"Yes. If you don't have your own blanket, they'll give you one, and it'll smell just like old socks. And no one will want to sit next to you because you'll smell like old socks, too."

"Nursery school couldn't be that bad," Anna Marie muttered. But she looked worried.

The blanket rolled itself up into a tight ball.

That afternoon, while Anna Marie took her panda for a wagon ride, the blanket began to sniff and whine.

"I guess I'm just an old rag," it blubbered. "An old rag ready for the garbage. No one ever really loved me."

"I've always loved you," Anna Marie
insisted. "And if you'd just listen, I
could tell you my new idea."
But the blanket wouldn't listen. It
rumpled itself up into a big lump.

Later on, while Anna Marie gave her doll a bath, the blanket began to pretend that it wanted to be alone.

"I'd much rather lie around the house by myself anyway," the blanket declared. "No more silly games. No more gooey kisses. No more sticky hugs. I'M GLAD."

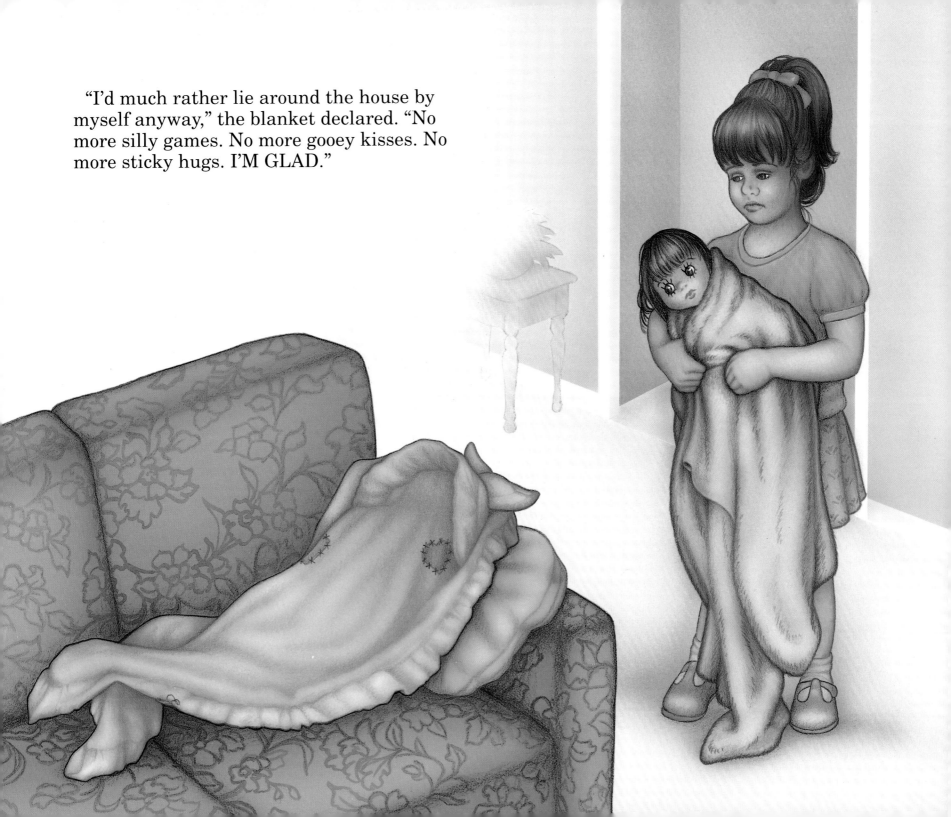

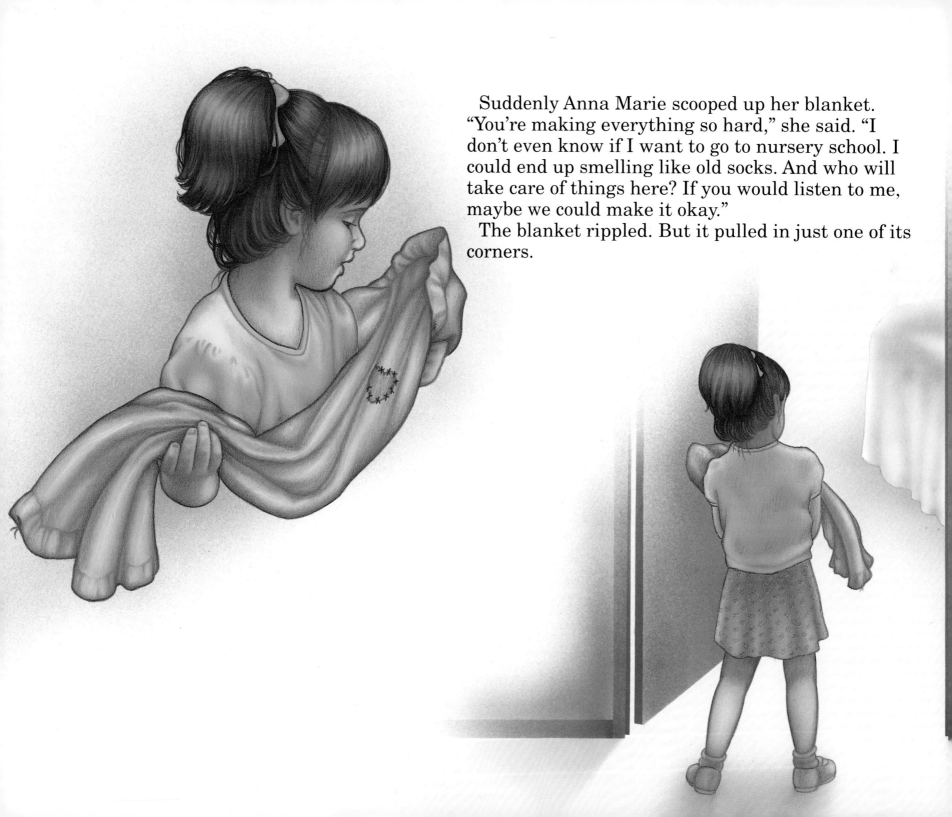

Suddenly Anna Marie scooped up her blanket. "You're making everything so hard," she said. "I don't even know if I want to go to nursery school. I could end up smelling like old socks. And who will take care of things here? If you would listen to me, maybe we could make it okay."

The blanket rippled. But it pulled in just one of its corners.

"I want to tell you my idea," Anna Marie
continued. "It's about a job. An important job."
The blanket didn't say anything.
"I want you to be baby-sitter for my babies," Anna
Marie announced. "I have a lot of them. I'll need
help once I start school."

"Banana the Monkey can be very naughty. He needs to be watched all the time.

"Whiskers Rabbit is always hungry. Someone has to make him a big lunch."

"Julie Panda likes to go for a wagon ride every afternoon.

"Molly Doll gets dirty all over. She needs a good bath before her nap."

"And they all need to be cuddled and snuggled and kept nice and warm. I won't be able to do it by myself once I start school."

"Will you help me?"

Anna Marie's blanket sniffled and coughed and smoothed its wrinkles. "Well," it said at last, "I certainly am the best blanket for the job. No one has cuddled or snuggled more than I have. I suppose I could try it—for a little while."

"Oh, thank you," Anna Marie said with a sigh of relief. She gave the blanket a hug. "I can show you everything you have to do. I have two days before nursery school starts."

The first day, Anna Marie showed her blanket how to keep one eye on Banana the Monkey all the time and how to make a big lunch for Whiskers Rabbit. She also taught the blanket how to take Julie Panda for a ride and how to give Molly Doll a bubble bath.

"You're very good at this," the blanket said to Anna Marie. "I hope I'll be able to do it as well."

The second day, the blanket showed Anna Marie a few special things that it knew how to do. The blanket spread out a picnic, wiped up a spill, and cuddled Julie Panda—*all at the same time*. It made up a game like hide-and-seek and blindman's buff—only better.

It gave the babies a nap-time swing that was just snug enough for good dreaming.

"I wish I could still nap like that," Anna Marie whispered.

That night was the last night before nursery school began.

"I know you're going to be a wonderful baby-sitter," Anna Marie told her blanket.

"I know you're going to love nursery school," the blanket replied. "You'll make lots of friends and play games and eat snacks. Nursery school is fun."

"Yes," Anna Marie decided, "it could be just like that."

"I should tell you something else," the blanket added after a moment. "I don't really think there's such a thing as a blanket that smells just like old socks."

That night, everyone slept very well.